Chinese Tale Series

中 国 神 话 故 事

Yu the Great Conquered the Flood

大 禹 治 水 net 119

Adapted by Ye Feng
Translated by Liu Guangdi
Illustrated by Ye Feng Jiang Ning

改编　叶　风

翻译　刘光第

绘画　叶　风　江　宁

DOLPHIN BOOKS
海 豚 出 版 社

First Edition 2005

ISBN 978-7-80138-565-9

© Dolphin Books, Beijing, 2005

Published by Dolphin Books
24 Baiwanzhuang Road, Beijing 100037,China

Printed in the People's Republic of China

According to the legend, a great flood ran wild all over China in the prehistoric times. The flood submerged the land of the country; people became homeless, running away from the disaster in all directions.

相传，在上古时期，中华大地上洪水滔天。洪水淹没了九州大地，人们无家可归，四处逃难。

Many people died from the flood and famine, and those who had survived became destitute and homeless, living a miserable life. Every place was filled with a dismal and sad atmosphere.

在洪水和饥荒中，人们大批死亡，活着的人流离失所，无家可归，苦不堪言，到处都弥漫着悲哀凄凉的气氛。

Having seen the people suffering, Emperor Yao, the ruler of the day, was determined to control the flood to save the common people.

当时的统治者尧看到百姓受苦受难，决心治理洪水，拯救黎民百姓。

Emperor Yao ordered a minister called "Gun" to control the water. Gun decided to use the "damming" method to control it.

尧让一个叫鲧的大臣去治理洪水。鲧决定用"围堵"的办法治理洪水。

There was a magic earth called "*xirang*" in the heaven, which could grow by itself without stop. One night, Gun sneaked into the heaven, and stole the *xirang* out.

天庭有一种叫息壤的神土，可以自己生长不息。一天夜里，鲧偷偷跑到天庭把息壤偷了出来。

Gun brought *xirang* to the place where the flood was the most monstrous, and he spread it to the ground. Then, *xirang* grew automatically, and it became a big and high dam immediately.

鲧来到洪水肆虐得最凶猛的地方，把息壤撒向大地，只见息壤自动生长起来，很快就变成了一座又高又大的堤坝。

The dam warded off the flood, and the saved people could not help cheering.

这座堤坝把洪水挡住了，得救的人们不禁都欢呼雀跃起来。

They returned to their homeland to build houses and cultivate their farmland, and began to lead a stable life.

他们重新回到自己的家园，建造房屋，耕种农田，开始过上了安定的日子。

God was very angry when he learned that *xirang* had been stolen. He ordered Zhu Rong, the God of Fire, to arrest Gun.

天帝得知息壤被鲧偷走，非常生气。他命令火神祝融去捉拿鲧。

Gun fought with Zhu Rong
drastically, and finally drove
Zhu Rong back to the heaven.

　　鲧和祝融拼杀得非常
惨烈，最后鲧把祝融赶回
了天庭。

The flood rose higher and higher, and finally overflowed
the dam, running wild on the earth again.

　　洪水越涨越高，终于漫过了堤坝，又开始在
大地上肆虐。

Gun felt very ashamed of his failure in flood control, so he committed suicide on Mount Yu.

鲧看见自己治水失败，非常惭愧，就在羽山自杀了。

After Emperor Yao died, his successor, Emperor Shun asked his ministers to control the flood again. When the ministers all looked at each other in despair, a youngster stood up, saying he would go to control the flood. The youngster was Yu the Great, son of Gun.

尧死后，继任君主舜命令大臣再去治水，但是人们都知道治水是一项非常艰难的工程，不敢承担任务，这时，一个少年站出来，说他愿意前往治水。这少年正是鲧的儿子大禹。

Then Emperor Shun commissioned Yu the Great to undertake the task.

舜便委任大禹来承担这项治水任务。

Yu the Great reached the riverside, and began to lead the people in their fight against flood. They split the mountain to remove earth and build a dam night and day, to stop the flood.

大禹赶到江边，开始带领人们与洪水搏斗。他们日夜不停地劈山填土，筑堤造坝，阻拦洪水的泛滥。

However,the water sprite made troubles
willfully, and damaged the human works,
making the flood go up continually.

但是水妖故意和大禹捣乱，破坏人
们的劳动，驱使洪水不断往上涨。

Yu the Great heard that a holy hermit called Meng in Mount Tu knew how to control the flood, so he went and looked for him.

　　大禹听人说涂山有一位高人叫做蒙，他有治住洪水的办法，便前往寻访。

Meng liked Yu the Great very much, so he offered him the Water Map he had treasured up for years.

　　蒙非常喜欢大禹，把自己秘藏的《水经图》送给了他。

Yu the Great fell in love with Nü Jiao, Meng's daughter, and later they got married.

大禹和蒙的女儿女娇相爱了，他们结了婚。

Shortly after the marriage of Yu the Great, the flood came again.

大禹结婚后不久，洪水又一次泛滥开来。

19

Yu the Great led the people in repairing the dam in spite of the tempest. After hard work of three days and three nights, the dam got repaired,so the flood was controlled temporarily.

大禹率领人们在暴风雨中抢修堤坝。经过三天三夜的努力，堤坝抢修好了，洪水暂时被治住了。

People went back home, hoping to live a peaceful and quiet life.

人们各自回家，希望能够过上太平日子。

At night, Yu the Great studied the Water Map carefully, in order to find out a new way to conquer the flood forever.

夜里，大禹仔细地研究《水经图》，希望能找到永久解决洪水的办法。

He consulted all the people, and decided to use the "draining" method to lead the water into the sea.

他集思广益，决定用"疏通"的方法，把洪水引入大海。

The huge water draining project began.

浩大的引水入海工程开始了。

The water sprite was very angry at the news. So he came with his soldiers and wanted to make troubles.

水妖得知后气急败坏，带着喽啰们来捣乱。

Yu the Great led the people fight against the water sprite, and finally drove them away.

大禹带领人们和水妖斗争，终于把它们赶跑了。

中国神话故事

In order to help Yu the Great, the kind-hearted river god brought his own green dragon and godly tortoise here.

为了帮助大禹，好心的河神带来自己的青龙和神龟。

The green dragon pushed
down the big mountain lying
in the way.

青龙把挡住道路
的大山卷倒。

The godly tortoise carried away
the earth and stones.

神龟把土石运走。

People worked hard together to dig ditches
and build dams with great enthusiasm.

人们齐心协力地开沟、
筑坝。大家的干劲十足。

For 13 years, Yu the Great had been busy at the construction site all the time.

在十三年的时间里，大禹一直在工地上忙碌。

Once he passed by his own house, he felt ashamed because he had not controlled the flood. so he did not enter his house.

　　有一次他经过家门口，因为还没有把洪水治好，觉得羞愧，没进家门。

For the second time when he passed by his house, he did
not enter either because of an urgent job.

　　大禹第二
次从家门前经
过，因为一件紧急的事
情，又没有进去。

For the third time, Yu the Great was on the way to the new worksite, passing by his own house again. He said to his wife, "Today, if you hear the drumbeat, please take the meal to me."

第三次，大禹要到新的工地去，他路过家门口，还是没有进去，只对站在门口的妻子说了句："今天，你听到鼓声，就把饭给我送来。"

At the new worksite, the stone was so hard that it remained intact no matter howhard the people smashed it.

在这个新的工地上，石头非常坚硬无论人们怎么砸，石头都岿然不动。

Yu the Great found out a new way, he changed himself into a big bear, and made all his efforts to smash the mountain, then the stones fell off one after another.

　　大禹想了一个办法，他把自己变成了一只大熊，使尽全力砸山，石块纷纷掉下来。

He dug and smashed all the day, and the rubbles on the mountain flew all around.

他不停地凿啊，砸啊，山上的碎石向四周飞去。

One piece of rock happened to fall on the drum at the foot of the mountain, making the drum sound.

碰巧有一块石头落在山下的鼓上面，鼓"咚"地响了一声。

When Yu the Great's wife heard the drum at home, she took the prepared food and went to the worksite.

大禹的妻子在家中听到鼓响，就带着准备好的食物往工地走去。

Yu the Great rushed to meet his wife when he saw her, but his wife suddenly saw a big bear rushing at her, and was frightened to death.

大禹见妻子走来就迎了上去，可是他的妻子猛然见到一只大熊朝自己扑来，立刻就被吓死了。

Yu the Great was very sad, and his tears dropped to his wife's body, turning her into a huge stone.

　　大禹非常难过，他的眼泪滴到妻子身上，妻子化作了一块巨石。

Yu the Great knew his wife was pregnant, and he shouted, "My child!" The huge stone split apart, and a boy was born. He was just the son of Yu the Great, named "Qi".

　　大禹知道自己的妻子有孕在身，他大喊一声："我的孩子！"只见巨石裂开，一个男孩儿出生了，这就是大禹的儿子——启。

After Yu the Great made arrangements for his son, he changed himself again into a big bear to hack the mountain to open up a new road.

大禹安顿好孩子，又变做大熊继续劈山开路。

The big mountain was cut through at last, and the billowy flood ran into the sea along the watercourse.

大山终于被凿通了，汹涌的洪水顺着河道，奔向大海。

Yu the Great did not accepted the "damming" method to stop the flood like his father, but adopted a "draining" method instead. The flood disappeared, and the earth was full of vitality again.

大禹没有像他的父亲鲧一样用"围堵"的办法阻挡洪水，而是采取了"疏通"的方法。水患消除了，大地重新呈现出一片生机。

中国神话故事

42

People began to live and work in peace and contentment from then on, and everyone was very grateful to Yu the Great for his efforts.

人们从此安居乐业，大家都非常感谢大禹的努力。

Because of the great achievements in water control, Emperor Shun summoned Yu the Great to his palace, greatly praising him, and gave the throne to him.

大禹因治水有功，舜把他召到宫里，对他大加称赞，并把王位让给了他。

Yu the Great, together with his son Qi, established the first dynasty of China, the Xia Dynasty, and his deeds have been respected and remembered by the Chinese people all the time.

大禹带着自己的儿子启建立了中国第一个王朝——夏，他的功绩永远被人们称颂与铭记。

图书在版编目　（CIP）数据

大禹治水 / 叶风改编；叶风等绘；刘光第译.
北京：海豚出版社，2005.10
　（中国神话故事）
ISBN 978-7-80138-565-9

　I. 大... II. ①叶... ②叶... ③刘... III. 图画故
事—中国—当代—英汉　IV. I287.8

中国版本图书馆 CIP 数据核字（2005）第 115073 号

中国神话故事

大禹治水

改编：叶　风
绘画：叶　风　江　宁
翻译：刘光第
社址：北京百万庄大街24号　　　邮编：100037
印刷：北京地大彩印厂
开本：16 开（787 毫米 × 1092 毫米）
文种：英汉　　印张：3
版次：2005 年 10 月第 1 版 2009 年 4 月第 4 次印刷
标准书号：ISBN 978-7-80138-565-9
定价：15.00 元